This book belongs to

_____

MINNIE'S SMALL WONDERS

Published by Advance Publishers
Winter Park, Florida

© 1997 Disney Enterprises, Inc.

Written by Suzanne Weyn   Edited by Bonnie Brook
Penciled by Don Williams   Painted by H.R. Russell
Designed by Design Five
Cover art by Peter Emslie
Cover design by Irene Yap

ISBN: 1-885222-86-6
10 9 8 7 6 5 4 3 2 1

innie Mouse rose with the sun, just as she did each morning she stayed on the farm. Quickly she got dressed and headed for the kitchen.

"Here, Fuzzy, girl," Minnie called as she filled the cat's bowl. "Come and get it!"

But Fuzzy was nowhere in sight.

"Fuzzy?" Minnie called from the porch. "Where are you?"

She walked to the field where a baby cow grazed by the fence. No Fuzzy here!

"Moo," said the little calf. Minnie noticed that the calf's wobbly legs seemed sturdier than when she was born.

In the horse pasture, Minnie kept searching for
Fuzzy. A baby horse nuzzled her hand. Minnie watched
as the foal ambled off to have his mother's milk for
breakfast.

Suddenly Minnie saw Mickey Mouse coming across the pasture. "Oh, good!" Minnie thought, clapping her hands together. "Mickey's good at finding lost things."

"Hi, Minnie," he called with a wave.

Minnie told Mickey about her missing cat.

"Don't worry," Mickey said. "We'll find her." He reached into his pocket and pulled out a magnifying glass. "Detective Mickey Mouse, on the case."

"Oh, Mickey!" she giggled.

"Let's look for clues in the barn," Mickey suggested.

Once inside the barn, Mickey checked all around for cat prints. "Baa!" the mother sheep warned. She didn't want anyone bothering her little lambs.

"Look, Mickey!" Minnie cried suddenly, pointing to the ground. "Pawprints! They're small, like Fuzzy's."

"Hmmm," said Mickey, following the prints out of the barn. "Very interesting."

The prints led right to Patches, the dog.

Mickey scratched his head in confusion. "These aren't Patches' prints," he said. "Her paws are too big."

"Patches' paws don't match the prints," said Minnie, "because these are puppy prints!" Patches' pups jumped up and licked Mickey.

"These little guys are almost eight weeks old," Minnie said as she petted the pups. "Soon they'll be ready to leave their mama."

When they moved on to the henhouse, Minnie stopped and listened. "No. Fuzzy isn't here," she sighed. "The chickens would be making noise if she were near because they're afraid of her."

Just then, a mother hen came along with her tiny chicks. "Eep! Eep! Eep!" they squeaked happily.

Several little goats, called kids, frisked around the yard nearby, climbing and jumping.

"They're all so cute," said Minnie sadly. "They remind me of my dear little Fuzzy. Wherever can she be?"

Mickey saw a small creature
nestled in the mud. "Look, Minnie,
I've got her!" he shouted.

"Oh, Mickey," Minnie said with a giggle.
"That's not Fuzzy. It's a piglet."

"Oops," Mickey said, blushing.

Next Minnie and Mickey walked into the woods. Suddenly Minnie stopped short. She'd heard something moving. "Listen!" she said.

"I hear it, too," Mickey said. "Maybe it's Fuzzy."

Minnie and Mickey peeked through the bushes, but they didn't see Fuzzy. Instead, they found Goofy and his son, Max, camping in the woods.

"Now, here's how you pitch a tent, son," Goofy instructed Max. "Just pull the tent back like so, and ..." *Boing!* The tent snapped, wrapping Goofy inside it. "Whoa!"

Mickey and Minnie climbed through the bushes and helped untangle Goofy.

"My cat, Fuzzy, is lost," Minnie told him. "We're looking for her here in the woods."

"Gawrsh, we'll help," Goofy said.

"Maybe Fuzzy climbed a tree," said Max.

"Golly, good thing I packed my brand-new, handy-dandy camping ladder," Goofy said. He began unfolding the ladder. It opened... and opened...and opened even more.

"Okay, son," Goofy said.

Max swallowed hard and started up the tall ladder.

16

Max climbed higher and higher until he found a nest of baby birds, chirping hungrily. One baby was bigger than the others. Max remembered that a mother cowbird lays her egg in the nest of another bird. The other bird parents often adopt the baby cowbird.

"Fuzzy's not up here," Max called back down to the others.

Suddenly, the ladder began swaying. Goofy had forgotten to hold it to keep it steady.

"Hold on, son!" yelled Goofy as he fumbled with the ladder.

"No, Goofy!" Mickey shouted. But it was too late.

Splash! The ladder landed in a woodland pond.
"I'm okay!" Max shouted to the others.

"Thank goodness," Goofy said with a relieved sigh.

"Hey, look at this!" Max cried. "A beaver dam!"

"And that looks like Fuzzy!" Minnie cried. "Oh, no!
Fuzzy hates water! I've got to help her!"

Minnie dove in, clothing and all. But as she got near, she saw it wasn't Fuzzy at all. It was a family of beavers teaching their two kits to swim.

The beavers dove down into the water. Thinking they might be leading her to Fuzzy, Minnie sucked in a deep breath and followed them.

The beavers swam up an underwater passage to their home of mud and twigs. When Minnie's head popped up above the water inside the beavers' home, she saw them huddled together, looking scared. "Gosh," Minnie thought. "I should have remembered that beavers are very shy."

Minnie swam back to her friends, who helped her wring out her wet skirt. Suddenly they heard a sharp snapping sound in the woods.

Goofy took out his camping guide. "It says here that if you hear a snapping twig, 'proceed with care.'"

Slowly, Goofy tiptoed through the bushes. He turned back to Minnie. "What color is Fuzzy?"

"Black and white," Minnie told him eagerly.

Goofy grinned. "Your kitty is saved!"

Goofy raced
through the bushes,
but suddenly came
to a screeching halt.
"Yikes!" he shouted.
"You're not Fuzzy!
You're a skunk!"

The skunk lifted her
tail and sprayed her
terrible-smelling spray
at him.

"It was a skunk," Goofy reported glumly.

"We can tell," said Minnie, smelling the skunk spray.

"She must have thought you were going to hurt her or her babies," Mickey said. "Spraying is a skunk's protection."

"Oh, my poor, sweet Fuzzy!" Minnie cried.

"Gosh, Minnie," Mickey said. "We'll find her."

Goofy read from his camping guide once again. "'Take a bath in tomato juice if you get sprayed by a skunk.' Gawrsh, Max, I better do that."

As Max and Goofy waved good-bye, Mickey saw a trail of broken branches. "An animal has been through here," he said. "Maybe it was Fuzzy."

Mickey and Minnie followed the trail to a clearing at the end of the woods. A lake glistened just beyond the trees. "I see something moving," said Mickey, as he ran ahead of Minnie.

"Look who's here!" he shouted.

It wasn't Fuzzy. It was Mickey's nephews, Morty and Ferdie, fishing at the lake.

"Hi, boys," Minnie greeted them. "We're looking for Fuzzy, my cat. Have you seen her?"

"No, but we'll gladly go look for her," offered Morty.

"Sure thing," added Ferdie. They put down their fishing poles and ran along the edge of the lake.

Ferdie ran so fast that he splashed by the edge of the lake. Whoops! He slipped and fell in. "Look!" he cried. "This lake is filled with tiny fish."

"They're not fish!" said Mickey, helping Ferdie to his feet. "They're baby frogs."

"They can't be," Ferdie argued. "They look like fish."

"Baby frogs look like fish at first," Mickey explained. "They're called tadpoles, or polliwogs. They'll slowly change while they grow. Then, in about six weeks, they'll leave the water as frogs."

Morty and Ferdie tried to help search for Fuzzy, but they soon began chasing colorful butterflies instead.

"I bet you don't know how a butterfly is like a frog," Mickey challenged his nephews.

"How?" asked Ferdie.

"Both animals go through metamorphosis! It means the animal changes its form and shape as it grows," Mickey explained. "A butterfly starts as a caterpillar. Then it builds a cocoon, and when it comes out, it's a butterfly."

Just then Mickey heard something in the bushes. Gently, he and the boys parted the branches. They saw something small and furry—it looked like a cat!

They all tumbled over one another as they tried to rescue Fuzzy. But it wasn't Fuzzy. It was a baby rabbit, called a kit. Minnie picked it up and cuddled it.

"It's getting dark," Mickey told Morty and Ferdie. "You two go straight home before it gets late."

After Morty and Ferdie had left, Mickey and Minnie remained in the woods and continued searching for Fuzzy. Still they couldn't find her anywhere.

As Minnie and Mickey walked through the darkening woods, something small and black swooped over their heads. "What was that?" Mickey cried.

"A bat," Minnie replied. "And she was carrying a baby on her chest. Bats are nocturnal. They only come out at night. I guess it's getting really late!"

"Hoo! Hoo!" With a flurry of wings, a father owl flew
from his family's nest. "He's going out to look for food,"
Minnie said, sounding worried. "What if he mistakes
Fuzzy for a rabbit? That's what owls eat."

"Fuzzy is fast and smart," said Mickey, but he was
worried, too.

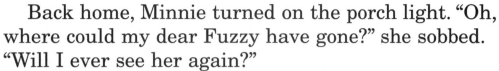

Back home, Minnie turned on the porch light. "Oh, where could my dear Fuzzy have gone?" she sobbed. "Will I ever see her again?"

"What's that sound?" Mickey asked.

Minnie listened. "It's coming from under the porch," she said.

Cautiously, Minnie looked under the porch. "It's Fuzzy!" she cried out happily. "Thank goodness."

Minnie heard squeaky little mewing sounds. "Well, what do you know?" she cried. "Fuzzy has a litter of brand-new kittens!"

"So that's why you were hiding, Fuzzy," Mickey said. "Kittens! How wonderful! They're so small!"

"That's just what they are," said Minnie. "They're small wonders."

Fuzzy nuzzled Minnie sleepily. It had been a long, exciting day for her. And for Mickey and Minnie, too!